Based on the TV series *Rugrats*® created by Arlene Klasky, Gabor Csupo, and Paul Germain as seen on Nickelodeon®

SIMON SPOTLIGHT
An imprint of Simon & Schuster Children's Publishing Division
1230 Avenue of the Americas
New York, New York 10020

First Simon Spotlight Edition, 1999

Printed in Mexico
10 9 8 7 6 5 4 3 2 1

Library of Congress Cataloging-in-Publication Data
Herman, Gail.
Pizza cats / by Gail Herman ; illustrated by Louie del Carmen and James Peters.
— 1st Simon Spotlight ed.
p.   cm. — (Ready-to-read)
Summary: After making a huge mess in the storeroom, Tommy, Chuckie, Phil,
and Lil persuade Pete to let three stray cats live in his pizza parlor.
ISBN 0-689-82391-6 (pbk.)
[1. Pizza—Fiction. 2. Cats—Fiction. 3. Toddlers—Fiction.]
I. Del Carmen, Louie, ill. II. Peters, James, ill. III. Title. IV. Series.
PZ7.H4315Pi   1999
[E]—dc21   98-42582
CIP   AC

Pizza Cats

By Gail Herman
Illustrated by Louie Del Carmen
and James Peters

Ready-to-Read

Simon Spotlight/Nickelodeon

Pizza time!
Tommy and his friends
looked for the box.

That's how they always
got their pizza—in a box.
But it was different tonight.
  "We're going *out* for pizza!" said Didi.

Didi and Betty took the babies
to Pete's Pizza.
Three stray cats were in the doorway.
   "Watch out for those cats,"
Didi told the babies.
"They might scratch."
   Lil did not think so.
They looked sad!
But Betty hurried
her away.

Inside, Pete was tossing pizza dough high in the air.

"Did you see those cats?" he asked Didi and Betty. "Someone should take them home. They are the biggest pests around."

SPE

9

The *biggest* pets?
Lil thought they were kind of small.
 The babies watched Pete
toss the dough.
Up and down.
Up and down.
 Suddenly Tommy whispered,
"Hey, guys, we have to find
the *real* pizza—the kind
that comes in a box!"

11

Tommy spied another room.
"That must be the place!" he said.
Didi and Betty were busy.
"Now's our chance," said Tommy.
"Come on!"
"I don't know, Tommy," said Chuckie.
"Anything can be behind that door . . .
anything!"
Then Lil and Phil took Chuckie's hands,
and they all sneaked away.

Inside the room, Chuckie kept
his eyes shut.
But the other babies grinned.
What a place!

The room was full of tomatoes
and big doughy balls.
"Come on, Chuckie," said Tommy.
"Let's play ball!"

The babies played catch with the dough and the tomatoes. *Splat!* Flour and bits of tomato flew everywhere.

"Look at this!" said Phil.

"It's the stuff we put on Christmas trees."

"Let's sprinkle it!" Lil said.

Just then, Tommy saw
the stack of pizza boxes.
"Pizza!" he yelled.
But the box was empty—
all the boxes were empty!

"No pizza anywhere!" said Tommy.

Then the babies heard a loud "*Mew!*"
Chuckie jumped.

"Wh-what was that?" he asked.

"It's the big pets!" said Lil.
"Maybe they want
to come inside."

How could the babies help?
Tommy had an idea!
The babies stacked the boxes
one by one,
all the way to the window.
Tommy climbed up
and let the cats in.

The cats looked around.
They nibbled on the tomatoes.
They chewed on the doughy balls.
"Look!" cried Lil. "The pets are
eating the toys!"

The cats rolled and played and ran and jumped with the babies.

"Now let's give the big pets a ride," Tommy said.

Around and around went the cats.

Crash! Boom! Bang!

"This is fun!" said Chuckie.
"Told you!" said Tommy.
Now what else could they do?

Just then, Pete, Didi, and Betty
hurried in.

"Oh, no!" cried Pete.
"Those big pests made a big mess!"
He was so upset, he
almost dropped
his pizza.

The babies looked at one another.
They felt bad.
They had helped to make
the big mess, too.

"Here, big pets," said Lil.
"You can play with these strings."
The cats batted the cheese,
and then gobbled it up.

"Why, they're just hungry,
the poor things!" cried Betty.

"*Mew, mew, mew . . . .*"
called the cats.

One cat licked some tomato sauce
from the pizza.

Another pulled at the cheese.

And one nibbled on the crust.

Pete smiled. "Well . . ." he said.
"The cats are kind of cute . . .
and they like pizza!
I guess they can stay here
where it's nice and warm,
and there's plenty to eat."

Didi looked at her watch.
It was getting late.
   "Oh dear," she said.
"Can we have the pizza to go?"
   The babies were happy.
The cats had a home,
and *they* would have
pizza in a box—
just the way
they liked it!